AT THE PIANO

J.S. BACH

Alfred EDITED BY
MAURICE HINSON

Illustration: Lianne Auk
Cover Design: Ted Engelbart

© Copyright MCMLXXXVII by Alfred Publishing Co., Inc.

CONTENTS

PAGE

FOREWORD

Johann Sebastian Bach. Painting by J. J. Ihle.

The keyboard music of J. S. Bach (1685–1750) is without equal in its quintessential combination of expressive depth, consummate mastery of formal procedures, counterpoint, harmony, melody, and masterful keyboard technique. The keyboard compositions are the center of his work. Bach's largest forms evolved from a concentration on the smallest details and their potential expressive power. His conception of musical composition is especially suited to keyboard style, for only a keyboard instrument provides immediately the spontaneous intimacy of improvisation and the possibility of polyphonic texture. Bach was a famous improviser, and improvisation thought out in peace and quiet was at the heart of his musical conception—free of the pressure of the occasions and circumstances for which the cantatas and some of the large chamber works were composed. Bach's keyboard music reveals with the greatest directness the process of his thought. It also bears the stamp of inevitability, the greatest single attribute of a composer, which means that each measure as it occurs sounds as if no alternate musical thought could have been conceived. Yet he indulged in varied versions (see the *Adagio* BWV 968, page 35 and the *Andante* BWV 964, page 38) that can be even more convincing than the original. If the greatness of a work is measured by the balance between overall form and the mass of detail which inhabits that form, then Bach is indeed preeminent in the art. His keyboard technique of writing is impeccable, his variety of mood inexhaustible, his feeling for the shape and duration of each piece is as perfect as it is possible to achieve. Bach is among those few geniuses who shine over all nations and all times.

BACH THE PERFORMER

Bach's fame during his lifetime was the result of his reputation as an interpreter. He was a performer in various roles—a choirmaster, and an interpreter on many instruments. He performed his own music, as well as the works of others. It is important to realize that Bach's scores were composed for his own use and often performed under his supervision in the various German towns where he was active as musical director.

Bach was by far the most outstanding organist of his day, and there were few who could rival him on the harpsichord. All who heard him were astounded at his improvisation and his complete ease and fluency at any keyboard. In 1738 Johan Matthias Gesner commented that:

> . . . either playing the clavier. . . with all the fingers of both hands, or running over the keys of [the organ] . . . with both hands and, at the utmost speed, with his feet, [he produced] by himself the most various and at the same time mutually agreeable combinations of sounds in orderly procession.

He also . . . remarked that Bach was "full of rhythm in every part of his body." Johann Adolph Scheibe, the year before, reacted similarly:

> One is amazed at his ability and one can hardly conceive how it is possible for him to achieve such agility, with his fingers and with his feet, in the crossings, extensions, and extreme jumps that he manages, without mixing in a single wrong tune, or displacing his body by any violent movement.

In an authoritative obituary presumably written by his son C. P. E. Bach, we have this statement:

> How strange, how new, how beautiful were his ideas in improvising. How perfectly he realized them! All his fingers were equally skillful; all were capable of the most perfect accuracy in performance. He had devised for himself so convenient a system of fingering that it was not hard for him to conquer the greatest difficulties in the most flowing facility. Before him the most famous clavier players in Germany and other lands had used the thumb but little.

Bach and his son, C.P.E. Bach, did more than any other to establish the function of the thumb in its pivotal capacity in our modern scale and arpeggio fingerings. C.P.E. Bach gave his father full credit:

> My late father told me about having heard great men in his youth who did not use the thumb except when it was necessary for large stretches. Since he lived at a time in which there gradually took place a quite remarkable change in musical taste, he was obliged to think out a much more complete use of the fingers, and especially to use the thumb (which apart from other uses is quite indispensable especially in the difficult keys) in such a manner as Nature, as it were,

wishes to see it used. Thus it was raised suddenly from its former idleness to the position of the principal finger.

Johann Nicolaus Forkel (1749–1818) wrote the first important biography of J. S. Bach in 1802. He describes Bach's finger technique as follows:

According to Sebastian Bach's manner of placing the hand on the keys, the five fingers are bent so that their points come into a straight line, and so fit the keys, which lie in a plane surface under them, that no single finger has to be drawn nearer when it is wanted, but every one is ready over the key which it may have to press down. What follows from this manner of holding the hand is:

(1) That no finger must fall upon its key, or (as also often happens) be thrown on it, but only needs to be *placed* upon it with a certain consciousness of the internal power and command over the motion.

(2) The impulse thus given to the keys, or the quantity of pressure, must be maintained in equal strength, and that in such a manner that the finger be not raised perpendicularly from the key, but that it glide off the forepart of the key, by gradually drawing back the tip of the finger towards the palm of the hand.

(3) In the transition from one key to another, this gliding off causes the quantity of force or pressure with which the first tone has been kept up to be transferred with the greatest rapidity to the next finger, so that the two tones are neither disjoined from each other nor blended together.

Continuing his description, Forkel wrote:

Sebastian Bach is said to have played with so easy and small a motion of the fingers that it was hardly perceptible. Only the first joints of the fingers were in motion; the hand retained even in the most difficult passages its rounded form; the fingers rose very little from the keys, hardly more than a shake [trill], and when one was employed, the other remained quietly in its position. Still less did the other parts of his body take any share in his playing, as happens with many whose hand is not light enough.

A person may, however, possess all these advantages, and yet be a very indifferent performer on the clavier, in the same manner as a man may have a very clear and fine pronunciation, and yet be a bad declaimer or orator. To be an able performer, many other qualities are necessary, which Bach likewise possessed in the highest perfection.

The natural difference between the fingers in size as well as strength frequently seduces performers, wherever it can be done, to use only the stronger fingers and neglect the weaker ones. Hence arises not only an inequality in the expression of several successive tones, but even the impossibility of executing certain passages where no choice of fingers can be made. Johann Sebastian Bach was soon sensible of this; and, to obviate so great a defect, wrote for himself particular pieces, in which all the fingers of both hands must necessarily be employed in the most various positions in order to perform

them properly and distinctly. By this exercise he rendered all his fingers, of both hands, equally strong and serviceable, so that he was able to execute not only chords and all running passages, but also single and double shakes [trills] with equal ease and delicacy. He was perfectly master even of those passages in which, while some fingers perform a shake, the others, on the same hand, have to continue the melody.

BACH THE TEACHER

We are not sure how much teaching Bach did at the harpsichord and clavichord but we know he took private students. His most famous students were his children Carl Philipp Emanuel and Wilhelm Friedemann. The *Little Clavier Books* for Anna Magdalena Bach (his second wife) and Wilhelm Friedemann provide ample evidence that he believed in thorough musical preparation:

Forkel tells us:

The first thing he did in his keyboard lessons was to teach his pupils his own kind of touch, of which we have spoken before. For this purpose, he made them practice, for several months on end nothing but single phrases for all the fingers of both hands, with constant regard to this clear and clean touch. After some months, none could get excused from these exercises; and, according to his firm opinion, they ought to be continued, at least, for from six to twelve months. But if he found that anyone, after some months of practice, began to lose patience, he would be so obliging as to write little connected pieces, in which those practice phrases were combined together. Of this kind are the six little Preludes for Beginners, and still more the fifteen two-part Inventions. He wrote both down during the hours of teaching, and, in doing so, attended only to the momentary need of the scholar. But he afterwards transformed them into beautiful, expressive little works of art. With his exercise of the fingers, either in single passages or in little pieces composed on purpose, was combined the practice of all the ornaments in both hands.

In the *Clavier Book for Wilhelm Friedemann*, begun on January 22nd, 1720 for his nine-year-old son, Bach provided a systematic, pedagogical keyboard method, beginning with an explanation of the clefs, the names of the notes, and principles of keyboard fingering. Here, J.S. Bach appears in the role of teacher and father. It would not be difficult to argue that Bach was the most self-consciously pedagogical of all the great composers.

TEACHING THE PIECES IN THIS COLLECTION

Since the performance of Bach's keyboard music on the piano has been the subject of controversy as well as a source of misunderstanding, the student who is studying the pieces in this collection should know something of the character and possibilities of the clavichord and harpsichord, the instruments for which this music was originally designed. The information concerning these instruments would help clarify the student's concept of the music. Musical thought could then evolve while technical powers were being developed.

The student should work on: 1) developing a technique of strength and complete independence of each finger; 2) a wide variety of *staccato*, plus a dependable *legato*; 3) quick changing of fingers on the same key; and, 4) a fast foot for pedaling. It is also necessary for the student to learn to think musically in terms of lines (horizontally) since this music is frequently a series of separate lines. These lines (voices) must be recognized and heard separately (horizontally, melodically), and then together (vertically, harmonically). Only the keyboard performer is in a position to appreciate the movement of the lines, their blending and their separation, their interaction and their contrasts. The piano's capacity for completely flexible shading is very useful for the clear projection and separation of these lines (voices).

Motives and figures must be identified and choreographed (characterized) since each of Bach's compositions is built on the foundation of one or more musical ideas (motives or figures).

1. Play the lines, motives and figures separately:

March in D Major, BWV Anhang 122, measures 1–4 (page 18)

2. **Analyze the rhythms:** varied note values in the right hand; pattern of quarter notes in the left hand.

3. **Analyze the melody:** look at the internal movement—left hand is exact repetition in bar 2 of bar 1, descends in bar 3 and has octave skips in bar 4; right hand has skip in bar 1, rising diatonic fill-in leads to bar 2, eighth notes in a rising scale from b to a and descends to e in bar 3.

4. **Analyze the harmony:** the harmonic implication of these four bars shows a tonic feeling in the first three bars and a strong cadence on the tonic in bar 4.

In Bach's music each voice has to sing its own melody, and the greater the number of voices, the richer the composition. "Voice-wise," rather than "hand-wise" thinking is characteristic. Therefore voices may pass freely from one hand to another and passages may be subdivided between hands at will.

This type of careful style analysis is a major tool in understanding Bach performance and will help the student to know what he/she should interpret and how to play it with a genuine sense of conviction.

In approaching Bach's keyboard music we should remember that this music has its own value apart from any instrument, even when the instrument was chosen by Bach. Even though the piano is one of the best possible instruments for Bach's keyboard music, its sound should not be the final goal of the interpreter, but only a helpful means of conveying this music which is independent of any instrument. Indeed, Bach's music is not instrumental, it is music itself. . . just music.

Johann Sebastian Bach.
Painting by E.G. Haussmann.

PLAYING BACH ON THE PIANO

Although written for keyboard instruments other than the piano (which was not yet well developed at that time), Bach's keyboard music must be regarded first and foremost as great music, transcending as his works so often did, any fixed medium of presentation.

One can only guess at Bach's probable attitude to our modern concert grand. However, his general openmindedness and readiness to experiment make it unlikely that he would have disapproved; we have his declared interest in Gottfried Silbermann's continued improvement of the action and tone of the early pianoforte to support this opinion. And while it is undeniable that a fine harpsichord and/or clavichord player can suggest a singing quality in his/her playing, it is surely possible for the pianist to prefer (i.e., in the *Adagio*, BWV 968, page 35) the modern instrument in fulfilling Bach's expressed wish for a *"cantabile style"*. We must not be accused of "romanticizing" Bach if we argue that warmth of feeling must have been present in the performances of players of his day and that the piano offers a broader scope for such warmth.

A major problem in performing Bach is that of giving a clear account of the progression of the individual voices of a contrapuntal texture. In this respect the pianist can, through his/her touch, influence and distinguish the tone of each voice to an extent not available to the harpsichordist; even when different stops are used by the latter for two voices which cross each other, it is difficult to avoid some confusion. Actually, each instrument has its dangers: one may hear in the piano careless pedaling, and in the harpsichord the indiscriminate use of octave couplings which make voice leading obscure.

Because of its wide range, unique sound quality and the infinite possibilities of voicing and shading, the piano is an ideal instrument to use in performing many of Bach's keyboard works. A piano with a bright timbre is more suitable for Bach than one with a sweet but velvety tone quality. The pianist should utilize the resources of the piano to point out, as best he/she can, the logical and structural elements of a Bach composition, while doing his/her best to refrain from uncalled for, exaggerated effects.

What constitutes good Bach performance is a question asked by many conscientious piano teachers and performers. There is no single universally accepted concept of good Bach performance, but the following interpretative information is provided to assist the pianist in arriving at a tasteful and artistic performance of Bach's keyboard works, based on efforts to bridge the chasm between baroque practice and contemporary musical communication. You will inevitably play Bach your way, but never cease to search for what might have been his, and to relate your own to it.

INTERPRETATION

Conceptions and interpretations of great Bach performers often vary, for there is a strong difference between the precepts and viewpoints of some of the great teachers of "schools" of Bach interpretation. Anyone who has heard a sufficient number of representative Bach concerts in Germany knows that there are at least two distinctly different schools of Bach interpretation—the objective and the subjective. The objective school follows with strict allegiance the meager directions of the score for tempo and dynamics. Each detail of the polyphonic texture and instrumentation is adhered to with utmost fidelity. The subjective school, in contrast, allows considerable deviation from Bach's original directions, from what is actually written down in the symbols and marks of Bach's notation. Dynamics and phrasing are added (and pedal when the piano is used in performance).

This editor feels that Bach's music should be played on the piano since this instrument incorporates some of the best qualities of the harpsichord and clavichord plus its own unique characteristics. The piano is an ideal instrument to convey Bach's musical thought, as long as the performer is aware of both schools of interpretation. We must ultimately realize that there is no single universally accepted concept of good Bach interpretation.

Some of the most important principles in the interpretation of Bach are discussed below.

TEMPO AND CHARACTER

The correlation between tempo and character (mood) is fundamental. Composers of the eighteenth-century used terms having the meaning of both *tempo* and *character*. Tempo markings seem to indicate more the effect of a specific tempo than the tempo in the sense of the speed; and character markings are used as often as, or more often than, simple *slow* or *fast* indications.

In this edition, Bach's tempo and character marks are identified and placed where he placed them, usually at the beginning of a movement or formal section of a movement. Bach used 45 tempo and/or character designations in his total output. There is good historical reason to believe that Bach regarded *allegro* (happy, merry, quite lively or awake) as representing the normal tempo—the *tempo ordinario*. For Bach, the slow end of the tempo spectrum was generally represented by *adagio* (at ease), not *largo*, and the fast end by *presto* (quick). Bach's six most often used (25 or more times) tempo designations, arranged (as he used them) in their proper sequential order of increasing velocity would be: *adagio, largo, andante, allegro, vivace,* and *presto.*

The following quotations from historical treatises reveal that performers in the Baroque period found signs within the pieces themselves to guide the determination of tempo and touch.

> The pace of a composition . . . is based on its general content as well as on the fastest notes and passages contained in it. Due consideration of the factors will prevent an *allegro* from being rushed and an *adagio* from being dragged.[1]

> "Brisk *allegros*" are meant to be played with emphasis on the detached notes, "tender *adagios*" are meant to be played with the broad, slurred notes. Close intervals suggest *legato*; distant jumping intervals are generally detached or played staccato.[2]

> Every piece of music contains at least one phrase from which it is possible to determine with certainty the type of movement most appropriate to the piece . . . one has to find out from the piece itself, and here one will infallibly recognize a true connoisseur.[3]

> Another indication . . . is the word to be found at the beginning . . . *Allegro non tanto . . . adagio* . . . all these words, unless used thoughtlessly, severally demand a particular expression.[4]

This last quotation reminds us that surely in Bach's time, Italian terms implied mood, character and expression rather than only tempo. The title of a piece may serve as a guide to tempo and interpretation. The editor reminds the performer that there is much information available regarding the tempo, mood and style of such compositions having generic titles like *minuet, polonaise,* etc. Indeed, one of the principal aims of **At the Piano with Bach** is to provide such information in an easily accessible format.

There is a significant difference between tempo determining character and, conversely, character determining tempo. The prevailing tendency in my editorial policy is to allow character to determine tempo, i.e., the conception of character preceded the conception of tempo.

[1] C.P.E. Bach, *Essay on the True Art of Playing Keyboard Instruments*, p. 151.

[2] Ibid.

[3] Leopold Mozart, *Versuch einer Grundlichen Violinschule*, p. 108

[4] Johann J. Quantz, *On Playing the Flute.* Translated by Edward Reilly, pp. 109-110.

Rubato

According to most Baroque sources, strict tempo was the general rule, and rhythmic liberty was the exception. Particularly in contrapuntal writing, the interrelationship of the parts makes the use of *rubato* (robbed time) disruptive; however, the pianist should make a slight *caesura* (break) before important entries of the theme or subject, to call attention to the return. The performer should also make a slight ritard on the final cadence of a piece. A subtle, discreet use of *rubato* is allowed only after the performer has acquired complete control of the rhythm, and a sense of style relating to the appropriate use of slight rhythmic fluctuations. In any case, *rubato* should be limited, for the incorrect application or overuse of this tempo deviation can result in an excessively romanticized interpretation.

FINGERING

"The true art of playing keyboard instruments depends on three factors . . . They are: correct fingering, good embellishments, and good performance . . .[5]

C.P.E. Bach places fingering first in listing the most important factors in playing keyboard instruments. Correct fingering is vitally important in contrapuntal pieces, which can hardly be performed with haphazard fingerings.

Bach left us two examples of his fingering practice in W. F. Bach's notebook of 1720. The *Applicatio* (BWV 994) shows us that for predominantly white keys he, like Rameau (in his 1722 treatise), considered some of the old scale fingerings indispensable. The crossing over and under of fingers in succession allows the performer to accent strong beats or maintain a smooth *legato* when two voices are played in one hand.

Applicatio, BWV 994, measure 2.

Measures 7–8.

Elsewhere in Friedemann's notebook, a fingered *Praeambulum* (BWV 930) shows that broken chords might often be treated as if unbroken.

Praeambulum, BWV 930, measures 8–10.

[5] C.P.E. Bach, *Essay*, p. 30.

The Use of the Thumb

Bach used the thumb more widely than his predecessors but even he used it very little when compared with its usage today. I have used the thumb considerably in this edition, especially where it supports contrapuntal phrasing. Much of the editor's fingering makes it possible to play *legato* without use of the pedal. This fingering should be ignored whenever *legato* is not desired and/or whenever an easier fingering is found. Bach specifically expressed a desire for a *legato, cantabile* style (in the sub-title of the *Two-Part Inventions*), however, the examples of his own fingering imply a much choppier phrasing than is sometime thought. This contradictory evidence should lead us to trust the music and decide on each individual case.

Bach's first biographer, Forkel, never heard Bach play, but he made a thoughtful synthesis of information received from people who had. He said that Bach's playing differed from that of his contemporaries in that he had found a "middle path" between too much *legato* and too much *staccato*, and thereby achieved the highest degree of clarity in his touch, relying upon a "light, unforced movement of the fingers" for what must have been a fairly constant, though effortless, *portato*. In general, the five fingers would be bent (*gebogen*) so that the fingertips "come into a straight line," but actually in playing each note Bach would apply a gradual drawing back of the fingertips, which would then "glide off the near part of the key" so that its discreet pressure would be transferred with the greatest rapidity to the next finger. The object of all this was to achieve the highest degree of clarity in the playing.

It has often been taken for granted that the technique outlined in the chapter on fingering in C.P.E. Bach's *Essay* was simply that of his father. His own claim was more discreet; he did not say of his father's technique "I shall expound it here,"[6] but rather, "I take it here as a basis:"

> Indeed, keyboard instruments were not tempered the same as nowadays, so one did not use all twenty-four keys as [we do] today, and therefore also one did not have the [same] variety of passages . . . My late father told me of having heard, in his youth, great men who did not use the thumb except when it was necessary for large stretches. Now as he lived at a time when gradually a quite particular change in musical taste took place, he was obliged thereby to think out a much more complete use of the fingers [and] especially to use the thumb—which among other good services is quite indispensable chiefly in the difficult keys—as Nature so to speak wishes to see it used. Thus was it raised at once from its former inactivity to the place of principal finger. Since this new fingering is so constituted that with it one can easily bring out every possible [thing] at the proper time, therefore I take it here as a basis.

[6] Ibid, p. 42.

The ultimate determinants of fingering should be linear independence, touch, phrasing, and comfort.

For the pianist playing the pieces in this collection, the fingering is based on two criteria: ease of reaching the keys, and ease of playing them with the correct touch. This implies that proper fingering demands *in advance* a conception of the phrasing as well as pedal usage that provides the desired sonority.

Good Bach performance requires a strong trill technique, and nothing loosens the fingers better than the trill. The fingering 5–3 is more reliable than 5–4 with ornaments that require the use of the fifth finger, and I have generally used this fingering.

PHRASING, ARTICULATION, AND TOUCH

Common phrasing practices in Baroque music include the following: 1. Phrases do not ordinarily end exactly at the bar line, but continue to a point within the measure. 2. With the exception of major cadences, the voices generally begin and end their phrases at different points. 3. If a particular musical idea (figure, motive) is stated several times, the phrasing is usually the same for successive statements.

C.P.E. Bach suggests the following means of determining the content of phrases:

> Above all, lose no opportunity to hear artistic singing. In so doing, the keyboardist will learn to think in terms of song. Indeed, it is a good practice to sing instrumental melodies in order to reach an understanding of their correct performance.

Those who follow this helpful procedure will find that the points at which one feels the desire to take a breath are often the junctions at which one phrase ends and another begins.

In J. S. Bach's keyboard works, occasional signs are used to indicate the articulation he preferred. In the *Two-Part Inventions*, slurs are found in No. 12, the A major Invention, in measures 19 and 20 as follows:

Two-Part Invention No. 12, BWV 783, measures 19–20

This was one of the common Baroque methods of articulating consecutive eighth-notes in triple meter.

The presence of "steps and skips" in the lines is also indicative of articulation. When notes proceed in stepwise, or conjunct motion, they are often connected as a unit; however, disjunct movement following a conjunct section often implies that a slight break should be made at the end of the conjunct unit.

Articulation consists of more than only *legato* and *staccato*: there are many subtle and fine shades in between. Regardless of shading or phrasing, articulate every note with great distinctness. Every note is important and you must not lose a single one. If a long held note fades away before its notated length, strike it again unobtrusively—that is better than losing it. The piano is capable of many varieties of articulation and phrasing. Many times a combination of different articulations is required simultaneously, as in the beginning of the *Adagio*, (BWV 968) on page 35, where a *legato* right hand should float effortlessly over a *portato* left hand that punctuates both the rhythmic and harmonic implications.

Strike the keys firmly but not percussively; do not pound or hammer. Raise the fingers for your strokes but descend lightly.

Phrasing should correspond with basic harmony. Do not separate portions of one harmony and then connect portions of two different harmonies.

STRUCTURAL CONSIDERATIONS

Many of Bach's keyboard works are written in sectional form. They develop motives, subjects, and/or figures that lead to section points at cadences, usually in near-related keys. If these section points are not made evident, there is a danger that the whole composition will become an endless and aimless maze of notes. Boredom and fatigue for performer and audience can result from performances of Bach's music that fail to establish structural landmarks in the form of section points. Bach's sectional cadences are carefully devised so as not to give the impression of total finality, but rather to suggest that the end is not yet, that more is still to follow. Careful control must be exercised so that a *ritard* leading up to a section cadence be definite but not excessive, that the movement be immediately resumed the moment the cadence is reached. It is also wise immediately to change the dynamic level after a cadence, to start the new section suddenly quieter or suddenly louder in order to show the occurrence of a new idea, or a new development. Notice the slight *ritard* in the following example, *Fugue in G major*, BWV 884 (see below), at the cadence in measure 22, and the *a tempo* on the second sixteenth-note in measure 23. The dynamic level also changes quickly in measure 23.

We know that throughout the late Baroque period, playing in a detached or *non-legato* manner was the accepted style. This type of touch was not usually notated as such. In 1755 Friedrich Wilhelm Marpurg wrote:

> A half arc . . . means that the notes are to be slurred. Now 'to slur' means not to lift the finger from the preceding note until one touches the next [note] . . . Detachment is the opposite of slurring; it consists of this: that one holds a note not for its [full] value, but only until about half [the value]. This is notated with [a] dot; Often one makes use of a little straight line for this . . . The ordinary procedure is opposed to legato as well as to staccato. In [this procedure], just before you touch the following note, you very quickly lift the finger from the preceding key. This ordinary procedure is never indicated [explicitly], since it is always presupposed.

DYNAMICS

Dynamics of both a gradual and terraced nature are appropriate to good Bach performance, but the pianist must guard against its excessive use. Although Bach's original instruments, with the exception of the clavichord, were incapable of gradations, such effects are desirable on the piano if not overdone. In addition to *crescendos* and *decrescendos*, the pianist may wish to use the *una corda* (left, soft) pedal to produce a change of color and timbre contrast. Such effects may be useful in approximating terrace dynamics, especially for echo effects or in repeated sections. Bach used 17 items to indicate dynamics, either single letters separately and/or fully written-out terms, in all of his works. They range from *forte* (strong, intense, but in a natural manner, without forcing the voice or instrument too much), to *piano* (in effect, soft; one should adjust or reduce the strength of the voice or instrument so that it may have the effect of an echo).[7] Bach also used the letters *pp*, contrary to our expectation, as reported by Walther to stand not for *pianissimo* but for *più piano*; and he used the written out term *pianissimo*. In the final chorus of his *St. Matthew Passion* (1736 version), Bach marked the final bars of the *B* section of the movement preceding the *da capo* (bars 76–9) with the

[7]J.G. Walther, *Musikalisches Lexikon oder musikalische Bibliothek* (Leipzig, 1732; facs. edition Kassel, 1953). Walther's *Lexicon* is a reliable guide to Bach's use and understanding of musical terminology. Bach and Walther were not only cousins but they were also in close musical contact. Bach acted as the Leipzig sales representative for Walther's dictionary.

Fugue in G major, BWV 884, measure 19-23.

following dynamic sequence: *piano-pp-pianissimo*. This passage clearly demonstrates Bach's use of graduated dynamics, for it amounts to a clear *decrescendo*. But the terms *crescendo* and *decrescendo* did not come into use until Jomelli used them in Mannheim, Germany, in 1757, seven years after Bach's death. This indicates the reason Bach did not use the term *decrescendo* in the *St. Matthew Passion* described before, for no term existed at the time to describe its effect.

But Bach left no dynamic indications in his solo keyboard and organ works. There are a few registration indications of *piano* and *forte* (manual changes) in the *Italian Concerto*, BWV 971, and a few echo-like *forte-piano* alternations in the Echo movement of the *French Ouverture*, BWV 831.

The main idea to remember when playing the pieces in **At the Piano with Bach** is to keep the dynamics within a reasonable level. This concept has always been observed with my editorial dynamics.

ORNAMENTATION

Ornamentation is an indispensable part of Bach's music. It influences not only the melody but all other aspects of the music. Bach wrote out a table of ornaments for his young son Friedemann. This table is not very exhaustive and so it is important to state a few basic principles for the performance of these and other ornaments found not only in the pieces in this collection but in other keyboard works of Bach. Embellishments must be performed correctly, but do not become overly anxious about them. If you open a new page in this book, and if your first worry is the ornaments, you are on the wrong track. It is a tragedy if concern for Bach's ornaments prevents you from realizing this music or enjoying it. Learn the pieces without ornaments to begin with, then add them and keep them in their proper degree of subordination. The following information should be of assistance:

1. Bach's ornaments are *diatonic*—i.e., they are to be played with the notes of the scale. Chromatic inflections alien to the scale are permitted only in case of modulation, or to avoid an abnormal interval. Augmented intervals cannot form part of an ornament; and ornaments comprised in a diminished interval—e.g., a chromatic turn in a diminished third—such as E flat, D, C sharp, D—are not acceptable unless fully written out by Bach.

2. Ornaments *belong to the time of the main note*. On keyboard instruments, ornaments and the notes or chords supporting them in the same hand must be struck *together*; if a chord is played arpeggio the ornament forms part of the arpeggio.

3. All ornaments, whether indicated by signs or by tiny notes, are subject to the beat, and must begin *on* the beat, not *before* the beat.

4. Trills ordinarily begin on the upper note.
   a) Trills on a note with a dot *stop at or near the dot*.

   b) Trills and mordents on a long note, when such note is tied to another and shorter note of the same pitch, *stop before* the latter, without emphasis and without closing notes (termination).

   c) The speed and the number of repercussions of trills and prolonged mordents is at the player's discretion and is determined by the tempo and the time value of the note on which it occurs. The termination of a trill, when not specifically indicated, may be added or omitted as the player chooses; traditionally, it is required at the end of an air or a large-scale instrumental piece.

5. Appoggiaturas may be short or long. When long appoggiaturas appear before notes divisible by two, take about half the value of the main note; before notes divisible by three, two-thirds. The duration of the appoggiatura depends upon the speed of the movement, upon the harmonic basis, and the prevailing rhythms. The appoggiatura is played on the beat with the accent *on the appoggiatura and not* on the principal note.

Capriccio (BWV 992) on the departure of brother Johann Jacob Bach (1706).

TABLE OF ORNAMENTS
from The Little Note Book for Wilhelm Friedemann Bach
(January 22, 1720)

"Explanation of divers signs, showing how to play certain ornaments correctly."

This table contains Bach's only written instructions about certain ornaments, and the fact that it is contained in a beginner's book is proof that he considered ornamentation a fundamental branch of knowledge.

	Written	Performed
Trillo		
Mordant		
Trillo and mordant		
Cadence (turn)*		
Doppelt cadence (turned trill)		
Idem		
Doppelt cadence and mordant		
Idem		
Accent steigend		
Accent fallend		
Accent and mordant		
Accent and trillo		
Idem		

Different symbols, performed alike

*Words in parenthesis indicate English equivalent.

Wilhelm Friedemann was ten years old when this Note Book was begun. This Table of Ornaments covers most normal problems, especially for a boy of that age.

The pianist who familiarizes him/herself with this ornament table, which indicates the correct realization of each sign, and then studies the way in which Bach used these ornaments, will be well on the way to developing a sense of the appropriateness of particular ornaments to each musical passage.

As Bach grew older, as we can easily see from the successive versions of his works, he tended to write out the ornaments in a fairly complete form—it was a contemporary complaint that he left nothing to the performer.

"Every ornament, every little grace, and everything that one thinks of as belonging to the method of playing, he expresses completely in notes."[8]

The essence of Bach's music lies in his more complete notation. Indeed, a great part of what we know about early eighteenth-century performance comes from Bach's fully notated scores.

Arpeggiation

The arpeggiation of solid chords was practiced during Bach's time. Begin all arpeggiation on the beat. When arpeggiation is used, the chord may be arpeggiated upward, downward, or depending on the desired length, rolled several times. Play the notes evenly, however fast they may be. The editor has suggested a few arpeggiations and has identified each one.

PEDAL

The correct use of pedal in Bach's keyboard works requires a knowledge of the style and an awareness of the mixtures and combinations of textures, both contrapuntal and homophonic. Highly critical listening is necessary as good pedaling is strongly dependent on the careful use of that faculty. The ears guide the feet in pedaling as the eyes guide the hands in reading at the keyboard.

The modern piano has three pedals, two of which may be used when Bach's keyboard music is played on this instrument. The damper (right) pedal should not be used to create extended sustained harmonic sonorities. Keyboard instruments in Bach's time had no damper pedal, and consequently, his compositions were conceived without the possibility of pedaling. But the pianist should use the pedal delicately and carefully in playing *legato*, even though this touch should usually be regulated by independent, controlled fingers. This pedal can help produce "the *cantabile* style of playing" Bach refers to in the preface of the *Two-Part Inventions*.

[8] Scheibe, 1737 (*The Bach Reader*, ed. Mendel and David, New York, 1966), p. 238.

Sometimes it is desirable to use the damper pedal to add resonance and color to the individual tones and chords.

In Bach's fast pieces it is better to refrain from using the damper pedal for the sake of clarity and transparency, with only rare exceptions. In his slower pieces, a finely syncopated pedal (usually about half-pedal) could be used for better *legato cantabile* and shading.

The *una corda* (left, soft) pedal may be used to change color, especially in repeated sections.

Construction of the piano makes it susceptible to certain pedal misuses on the part of the performer. For the pianist, the damper pedal is often used too extensively for Bach's style of keyboard writing, and the use of dynamic gradations is often overextended in terms of terrace dynamics of the Baroque period.

The way you use the pedal is more important than should or shouldn't you, but always aim for clarity.

ABOUT THIS EDITION

At the Piano with Bach is a performing critical edition aimed at helping the pianist perform this music in a stylistically acceptable manner. For many pianists, it is desirable to have suggested articulation, dynamic and fingering indications and realized ornaments. This gives the pianist a starting point in the process of learning Bach's performance style, and **At the Piano with Bach** aims to accomplish this in a practical and scholarly fashion.

I have used the *Neue Bach Ausgabe* (New Bach Edition) and the most reliable sources I could locate as the basis for this edition. All fingering, metronome marks, and dynamics are added by the editor as well as most articulation indications. I have used the comma (,) to indicate subtle articulation separations in a few of the pieces. But in terms of editorial markings, I have frequently indicated less rather than more to allow the performer his/her own freedom in some degree to create an interpretation of his/her own. Ornaments are realized either in the score or in footnotes. The editor hopes his discussion and additions are only enough to help make this music a living experience.

In this edition the piano is treated on its own terms, with full appreciation of its tonal resources, and particularly of its sustaining quality. All of the fine expressive qualities of the harpsichord and clavichord are utilized as effectively as possible. The harpsichord could play with brilliance and incisive rhythm—these qualities are available to the pianist also. Terraced dynamics, sudden shifts of level from *forte* to *piano* and back, can produce a wonderful musical effect. Dynamic shadings are also employed, using this outstanding quality of the clavichord.

The pieces of this collection are organized in order of progressive difficulty, beginning with a number of comparatively easy works, easy not only in a technical sense, but more importantly, in interpretative demands. They range in difficulty from early-intermediate through moderately advanced. The pianist could play some of the easy dances and little preludes as early as the end of the first year of study, and could use the collection through college and graduate school with such pieces as the *Adagio*, BWV 968, and the *Capriccio on the Departure of His Beloved Brother*, BWV 992.

BWV numbers refer to Wolfgang Schmieder's *Thematish-systematisches Verzeichnis der musikalischen Werke von Johann Sebastian Bach.* Leipzig: Breitkopf und Hartel, 1950. *Anh.* refers to the appendix of this volume.

ABOUT THE PIECES

ADAGIO IN G MAJOR, BWV 968
(after the Violin Sonata in C Major) *Page 35*
This single movement comes from Bach's third Violin Sonata in C major. Although they are identical compositions, Bach's keyboard version contains more fully realized harmonies, contrapuntal figures and ornamentation that make the keyboard piece one of his greatest slow movements.

ANDANTE IN F MAJOR, BWV 964
(after the Violin Sonata in D Minor) *Page 38*
This piece is the third movement of Bach's solo Violin Sonata in D minor, probably arranged by Bach for solo keyboard. It is a fine example of the widespread contemporary technique of arranging, and it also demonstrates how gratifying Bach's violin pieces could be when adapted for the piano. The arrangement equals or even transcends that of the original violin sonata. Indeed, Bach was passionately devoted to the art of transcription.

CAPRICCIO ON THE DEPARTURE OF
HIS BELOVED BROTHER, BWV 922 *Page 53*
This piece was written when Bach was 19, and is one of the freshest and most delightful works by the young composer. It has a naive, spontaneous humor that appears only rarely in Bach's later works; with its picturesque qualities, its tone pictures (the only example of program music by Bach), and its gaiety, it is the work of a young talent that could have

developed a much more popular manner. The occasion was the departure of his younger brother Johann Jakob to take a position as oboist in the band of Charles XII of Sweden. Johann Kuhnau's *Biblical Sonatas* may have been the model for this early work.

FANTASIA IN C MINOR, BWV 906   *Page 42*

This beautiful work contains Italian characteristics —i.e., the hand crossings—and an attractive rhythmic vitality. It was composed in Leipzig, Germany around 1738. The character is somewhat stormy, with the two voices running sometimes in contrary motion, and sometimes together—at other times they clash and intertwine. The form is an early sonata-allegro design, lacking only the return to the finely contrasted second theme (measures 9–13) in the recapitulation, to make a balanced exposition (measures 1–16), development (17–33), and a modified recapitulation (34 to the end, bar 40).

INVENTION NO. 8 IN F MAJOR
BWV 779   *Page 26*

The canonic imitations of this brisk and lively two-part invention provide numerous obvious opportunities for the performer. Bars 1–7 are a canon at the octave; bars 8–10 are a canon at the ninth; the ideas in bars 1–2 are developed in bars 12–20; the idea from bar 3 is developed in bars 21–25; bars 26–34 are bars 4–12 transposed to the tonic.

MARCH IN D MAJOR, BWV Anh. 122   *Page 18*

The character of this piece is joyful, and short *staccatos* will help convey this mood. Make careful distinctions between *p*, *mp*, and *mf*. Articulation and dynamics may be varied on the repeats if so desired.

MARCH IN E-FLAT MAJOR
BWV Anh. 127   *Page 22*

The mood and character of this charming piece seems to be one of kindness and friendship. Be sure the duplets following the triplets in measures 5, 6, 8, 13, 21, 24, 25, and 26, are absolutely accurate rhythmically.

MARCH IN G MAJOR, BWV Anh. 124   *Page 19*

The repeated notes should give the effect of a drum accompaniment to the trumpet-like melody. Make the articulation impressively clear.

POLONAISE IN F MAJOR
BWV Anh. 117a   *Page 20*

This piece is contained in the *Anna Magdalena Notebook* of 1725. The Polonaise uses repetition of short precise motives (measures 1, 2, 4, 5, etc.), and employs characteristic accompanying motives (here the bass chords). The character of this Polonaise is one of grandeur and majesty.

PRELUDE AND FUGUE IN G MAJOR
BWV 884   *Page 47*

This pair is No. 15 in Vol. II of the *Well-Tempered Clavier*. The prelude is in two (repeated) sections, the first leading into the dominant key and the second returning to the tonic. Keep the suave prelude graceful and not too fast. Light finger technique and rhythmic drive are essential. Humor bars 14–15 and 46–47 to be sure they are especially melodious. The fugue dances briskly in a 3/8 rhythm with a subject that is a garland woven from broken triads and seventh chords. Its length permits no serious working out. Bringing out the subject and little else is perhaps the most flagrant, and the most common fault in playing contrapuntal music. It is

Invention No. 8 in F Major, BWV 779. From *The Little Note Book for Wilhelm Friedemann Bach.*

never the subject which is of central interest in a fugue, but the way the subject is embedded in the polyphonic structure. The performer must always try and find a way to clarify the relation of the subject to its surrounding voices. The two-voice countersubjects (measures 16 forward, and 41 forward) must come through clearly. A dramatic bravura passage in thirty-seconds rolls across the keyboard at measures 62–64 and leads to the subject at measure 65, which appears for the final time in the middle voice. A graceful coda (measures 70–72) closes the fugue.

PRELUDE IN C MAJOR, BWV 846a   Page 28

This famous Prelude is here seen in its earliest form—in the W. F. B. Notebook. It is eight measures shorter than the final version that appears as Prelude I in the first book of the *Well-Tempered Clavier*. In this first version the broken-chord figuration stops at measure 7, and solid block chords are indicated to the end of the piece, although the performer is to continue the broken-chord figuration using the block chord harmonies. Give the final chords its full four counts and do not break the spell of the quiet ending by moving too soon. Hold the atmosphere!

PRELUDE IN C MAJOR, BWV 939   Page 17

Broken triads with phrasing across the bar line characterize this piece that probably had its origin in Bach's teaching. The mordants in measures 9–11 should be played by dropping the hand lightly without strong accent, since they are merely decorating the pedal point.

PRELUDE IN C MINOR, BWV 934   Page 24

This prelude is from the *Six Little Preludes*. The continuously flowing eighth-notes need careful control. The suggested phrasing (breath marks) adds "facial expression" and melodic character. The quarter notes should be played lightly non-legato throughout.

PRELUDE IN F MAJOR, BWV 927   Page 21

Each hand gets a careful workout in sixteenth-note figuration in this little prelude. Keep these sixteenths light and flowing. The *diminuendo* beginning in measure 11 should begin *forte*. Remember that *diminuendo* means "becoming quieter." Therefore, *diminuendo* implies *forte* at first, becoming quieter as the *diminuendo* gradually takes effect. Reversing this concept: *crescendo* means "becoming louder." Therefore, *crescendo* implies a quiet dynamic at the beginning, gradually getting louder.

PRELUDE NO. 6 IN D MINOR, BWV 851   Page 32

This prelude is from volume one of the *Well-Tempered Clavier*. It is built on a recurring triplet figure. The emotional quality of this piece is great if proper attention is given to the true phrasing of the triplet figure. In all bars, until the last three, it is vital to keep in mind that the triplets of each group should be thought of as:

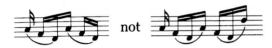

The repeated notes in the bass should be almost tied. At measure 15 the climax begins to build on a tonic pedal point and is arrived at in measure 24. The final chords should be arpeggiated from the bottom to the top.

PRELUDE NO. 16 IN G MINOR, BWV 861 Page 40

This strict three-voiced, arioso prelude is from volume one of the *Well-Tempered Clavier*. Its use of the trill, plus florid passages, give it a lyric beauty that is rare even with Bach. The trills in measures 1, 3, 7 and 11 begin on the main note. These trills should gradually accelerate like:

A slight breath after the first sixteenth note in measures 2, 4–6 and 8 is suggested. In measures 14–15 the bass should be well-marked. The final trill (measure 19) should end like:

This is a quiet, slow (eight pulses to the measure), but not dragging movement.

SINFONIA NO. 1 IN C MAJOR, BWV 787   Page 30

This cheerful contrapuntal "Three-part Invention" contains moving voices that go their own independent way, but fit together beautifully to form the whole piece. Be sure that all the notes are held for their full time value. Three voices are involved most of the time, and the performer should always be aware of the rich texture Bach has brought to this piece.

Maurice Hinson

PRELUDE IN C MAJOR

BWV 939

This piece is based on the earliest known source, a manuscript from the collection of Johann Peter Kellner.

MARCH IN D MAJOR

BWV Anh. 122

MARCH IN G MAJOR

BWV Anh. 124

POLONAISE IN F MAJOR

BWV Anh. 117a

Maestoso ♩ = 60

ⓗ Arpeggiate from the bottom upward.

PRELUDE IN F MAJOR

MARCH IN E-FLAT MAJOR

BWV Anh. 127

PRELUDE IN C MINOR

BWV 934

Allegretto espressivo ♩ = 120

INVENTION NO. 8 IN F MAJOR

BWV 779

ⓐ The first version of this piece, in W.F. Bach's Notebook, omits measures 17-20.

PRELUDE IN C MAJOR

Moderato ♩ = ca. 58

BWV 846a

SINFONIA NO. 1 IN C MAJOR

BWV 787

This edition is based on the autograph written by Bach in 1723 as contained in W.F. Bach's *Clavier-Büchlein*.

PRELUDE NO. 6 IN D MINOR

from
The Well-Tempered Clavier
Vol. I

BWV 851

ADAGIO IN G MAJOR
after the Violin Sonata in C Major

BWV 968

The mordents, indicated in measure one, may be used in similar rhythmic patterns (measures, 2, 3, 4, 8, etc.), at the performer's discretion.   In measure one, the pedal should be depressed at the point where the mordent is completed.

ANDANTE IN F MAJOR
after the Violin Sonata in D Minor

BWV 964

Cantabile ♩ = 44

PRELUDE NO. 16 IN G MINOR

from
The Well-Tempered Clavier
Vol. I

BWV 861

Andante cantabile ♪ = 88

FANTASIA IN C MINOR

BWV 906

44

ⓐ The autograph does not show mordents in measures 17, 18, 34 and 35, but they should be added.

ⓑ The mordent is missing in the autograph.

PRELUDE AND FUGUE IN G MAJOR

from
The Well-Tempered Clavier
Book II

Prelude

Allegro ♩ = 112

BWV 884

Fugue in 3 voices

S. = Subject

CAPRICCIO
ON THE DEPARTURE OF HIS BELOVED BROTHER
I. ARIOSO

BWV 992

His friends try to persuade him to abandon his journey

II. ANDANTE

They suggest accidents that may befall him

ⓐ Roll from the bottom upward.

III. ADAGIOSISSIMO*

Lamentations of his friends

* Bach indicated only the notes of normal size, i.e., the bass line and the melody of the right hand.
The small notes indicate one possible realization of Bach's figured bass.

*Arpeggiate from the top downward.

IV. ANDANTE CON MOTO

Seeing that it cannot be otherwise, his friends say good-by

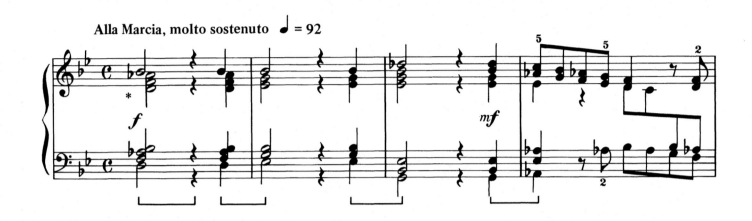

*The chords in the first three measures may be arpeggiated from the bottom upward.

V. ARIA DEL POSTIGLIONE

(Postilion's Song)

VI. FUGUE BASED ON THE POSTILION'S HORN CALL